OUTDOOR ADVENTURE

DUCK HUNTING

BY GEORGE PENDERGAST

Gareth Stevens PUBLISHING

HOT TOPICS

Please visit our website, www.garethstevens.com. For a free color catalog of all our high-quality books, call toll free 1-800-542-2595 or fax 1-877-542-2596.

Pendergast, George.
Duck hunting / by George Pendergast.
p. cm. — (Outdoor adventure)
Includes index.
ISBN 978-1-4824-1227-7 (pbk.)
ISBN 978-1-4824-0966-6 (6-pack)
ISBN 978-1-4824-1491-2 (library binding)
1. Duck shooting — Juvenile literature. I. Title.
SK333.D8 P46 2015
799.2—d23

First Edition

Published in 2015 by
Gareth Stevens Publishing
111 East 14th Street, Suite 349
New York, NY 10003

Designer: Nick Domiano
Editor: Ryan Nagelhout

Photo credits: Cover, p. 1 © iStockphoto.com/mauribo; cover texture Yuriy Boyko / Shutterstock.com; cover ribbon blinkblink/Shutterstock.com; pp. 4-5 Rubberball Productions/Vetta/Getty Images; pp. 6-7 Ana Gram/Shutterstock.com; pp. 8-9 Suzi Nelson/ Shutterstock.com; p. 11 Ron Chapple Stock/Thinkstock.com; pp. 12-13 MyLoupe/Universal Image Group/Getty Images; pp. 14-15, 22-23 Konjushenko Vladimir/Shutterstock.com; pp. 16-17 Teresa Levite/Shutterstock.com; pp. 18-19 Dmitry Kalinovsky/Shutterstock.com; pp. 20-21 Guido Bissanttini/Shutterstock.com; p. 24-25 Kirk Geisler/Shutterstock.com; p. 27 Linda Freshwaters Arndt/Photo Researchers/Getty Images; pp. 28-29 Michael Pearce/ Wichita Eagle/Getty Images p. 30 (shotgun) zimand/Shutterstock.com; p. 30 (duck) Jim Hughes/Shutterstock.com.

Printed in the United States of America

CPSIA compliance information: Batch #CS15GS: For further information contact Gareth Stevens, New York, New York at 1-800-542-2595.

CONTENTS

FUN WITH FOWL

Many people love to hunt. One of the best animals to hunt is the duck! Duck hunting is a great way to get outside and see nature. There's a lot to learn about duck hunting.

Ducks are birds that live in and near water. There are many different kinds. Ducks swim with their webbed feet. Ducks also belong to a larger group of birds called waterfowl.

BRINGING THE DUCKS IN

Duck hunters put fake ducks where they want to hunt. These are called decoys. The decoys are put where ducks usually land and feed. Some people make their own decoys!

DUCK CALLING

Hunters don't just wait for ducks to fly by. They bring the ducks right to where they are! Duck hunters use duck calls. Hunters blow into these calls to **mimic** the sounds ducks make.

Duck hunters have three main calls. The “hail” call attracts ducks to where the decoys are. Groups of ducks circle the **blinds** where hunters hide. The other calls, a “greeting” and a “feeding chuckle,” keep the ducks moving nearby.

COVER UP

Duck hunters need to find cover. Cover keeps ducks flying in the sky from seeing hunters. Some hunters lie on the ground and put **brush** and plants on top of themselves.

Many duck hunters climb up trees. Some hunters also build hunting blinds. Ducks like to land flying into the wind. Duck hunters take cover near their decoys in the direction the wind is blowing.

READY… AIM…

Hunters shoot at ducks as they spread their wings and are about to land on water. They aim about 6 to 8 inches (15 to 20 cm) in front of the ducks. Hunters use a gun called a shotgun.

If a hunter misses the duck while it lands, the noise from his gun will scare it out of the water. Duck hunters have another chance to shoot the duck as it flies away. Hunters need to work fast!

FINDING YOUR DUCK

After a hunter shoots a duck, he or she has to go get it. Finding the duck isn't always easy. Hunters often have to **wade** through water and mud.

DOGS CAN HELP!

Many people hunt with dogs! These dogs are called **retrievers**. They go out into the water and search for the fallen duck. A retriever snags the duck in its mouth and brings it back to its owner.

Training your dog for duck hunting is important. You can teach your dog to fetch or let professionals work with your dog at a **kennel**. Without a retriever, you might not find your duck!

Duck hunting is a great way to spend time with your family. You can even spend time with your pet. Make sure you're safe the next time you go duck hunting!

Duck Hunting Safety

- Always act as if every gun is loaded.
- Never point a gun at anyone.
- Don't put your finger on a gun's trigger until you're ready to fire.
- Don't leave equipment on the ground.
- Be sure of your target before firing.
- Always wear orange so other hunters can see you.

FOR MORE INFORMATION

Books

Carpenter, Tom. *Waterfowl Hunting: Duck, Goose, and More.* Minneapolis, MN: Lerner Publications, 2013.

Lambert, Hines. *Hunting Ducks.* New York, NY: PowerKids Press, 2013.

Omoth, Tyler. *Duck Hunting for Kids.* North Mankato, MN: Capstone Press, 2013.

Websites

Ducks Unlimited

ducks.org

Find out more about duck hunting, and learn where you can start hunting today.

DU Quizzes & Trivia

ducks.org/hunting/quizzes

Take these great quizzes to test your duck knowledge.

Publisher's note to educators and parents: Our editors have carefully reviewed these websites to ensure that they are suitable for students. Many websites change frequently, however, and we cannot guarantee that a site's future contents will continue to meet our high standards of quality and educational value. Be advised that students should be closely supervised whenever they access the Internet.

GLOSSARY

blind: a small building hunters hide in while they watch for animals

brush: short trees or twigs

kennel: a place where dogs are housed or trained

mimic: to make the same sound as something else

retriever: a type of dog that brings ducks back during a hunt

wade: to step in and through water or mud

INDEX